ROBERT
WALSER

ANSWER
TO AN
INQUIRY

PAUL
NORTH

FRIESE
UNDINE

UGLY
DUCKLING
PRESSE

Robert Walser:
Answer to an Inquiry

Translated by Paul North
Illustrated by Friese Undine

Ugly Duckling Presse
Brooklyn: 2010

WHENEVER HUMANS have progressed beyond the mere struggle for physical existence, there has been theater and the drive towards self-destruction. In 1907 the Swiss author Robert Walser wrote a brief outline of a performance of self-destruction. Stripped entirely of plot and characters, his sketch gives advice on how to convey anguish to an audience as well as practical tips on stagecraft. With this new translation by Paul North, we hope to expand upon Walser's ideas for the contemporary audience. Whether your performance is in a conventional theater, staged on the street or employs film or new media, this booklet should help both professionals and amateurs enact raw suffering in their chosen venue. It should be said, though, that without stage illusion or digital enhancement, this drama would be difficult to perform twice.

— FRIESE UNDINE

YOU ASK ME if I have an idea for you, sir, you ask me to draft a sketch, a play, a dance, a pantomime, or some other thing you could use, that you could depend on.

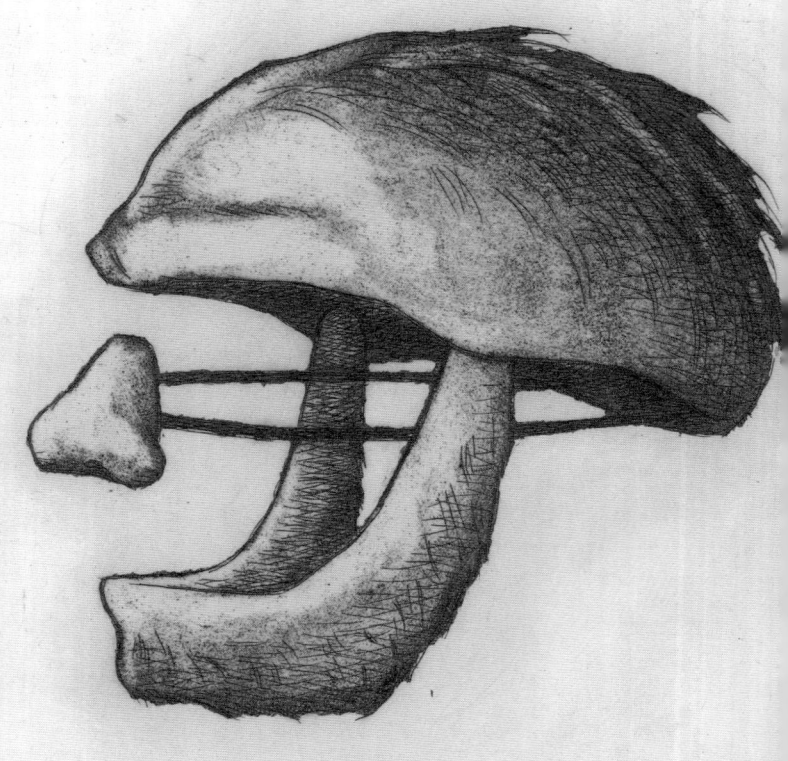

My idea is approximately the following:
get yourself masks, half-a-dozen noses,
foreheads, tufts of hair and eyebrows and
twenty voices.

If possible find a painter, one who is also a tailor, and have him make up a series of costumes;

take care that a couple of good solid pieces of
scenery are procured, so that, wrapped in
a black coat, you can go down a
stairway or look out a window
and let out a roar,

a short, lion-like, thick, heavy roar, such that people actually believe a soul is roaring, a human breast.

BEG YOU TO pay careful attention to
this cry, sir; put elegance into it, let it
resonate purely and correctly, and then
you are permitted, if you must,

to reach your hand for one of your tufts of hair,
in order to lay it *doucement* on the earth. The
effect of such a thing, when it is gracefully done,
is gruesome. They will think pain has made you
speechless.

To achieve a tragic effect one must seize both the nearest and the most extremely remote means;

I say this so you understand that now it will be good to stick your finger in your nose and dig around with it intently. Upon seeing this, many spectators will cry, upon seeing such a noble, melancholy figure as you behave in so ill-mannered and pitiful a way. It only really matters what face you make while doing this and from which side it is lit.

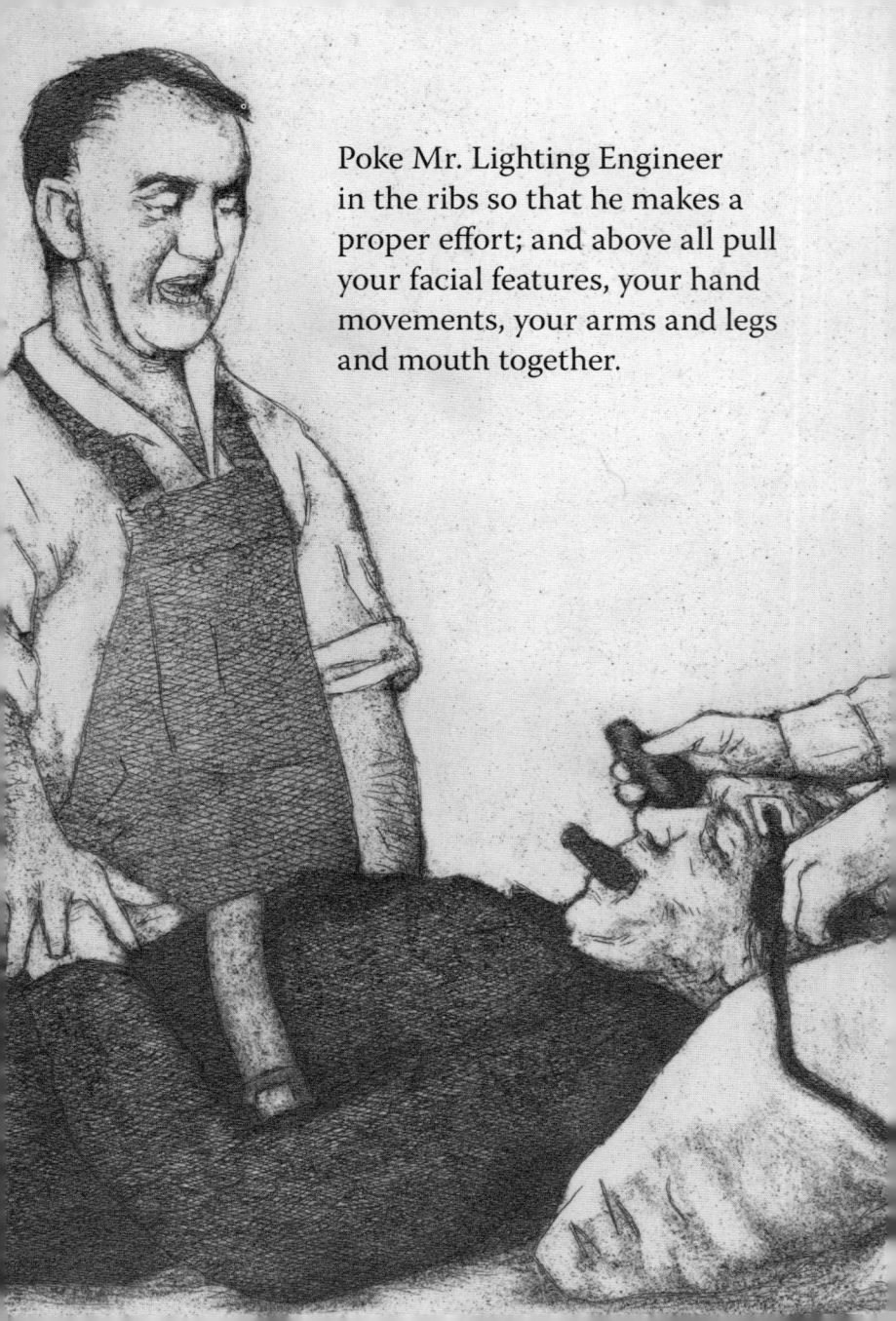

Poke Mr. Lighting Engineer in the ribs so that he makes a proper effort; and above all pull your facial features, your hand movements, your arms and legs and mouth together.

REMEMBER WHAT I told you once before, namely, that it is possible to perform fearsomeness, beauty, mourning,

or love, or whatever else you want merely by opening or closing one eye in one way or another.

It does not take much to act out love, but sometime in your godforsaken, savagely tattered life you must have honestly and simply felt what love is and how love likes to behave.

Naturally, it is the same with anger,
with the feeling of anonymous mourning,
in short, with every human sentiment.

By the way, I advise you to practice gymnastics often in your room, to go to the woods and strengthen the lobes of your lungs, to do sports, but with distinction and good measure, to go to the circus and observe the manner of Dumb August,

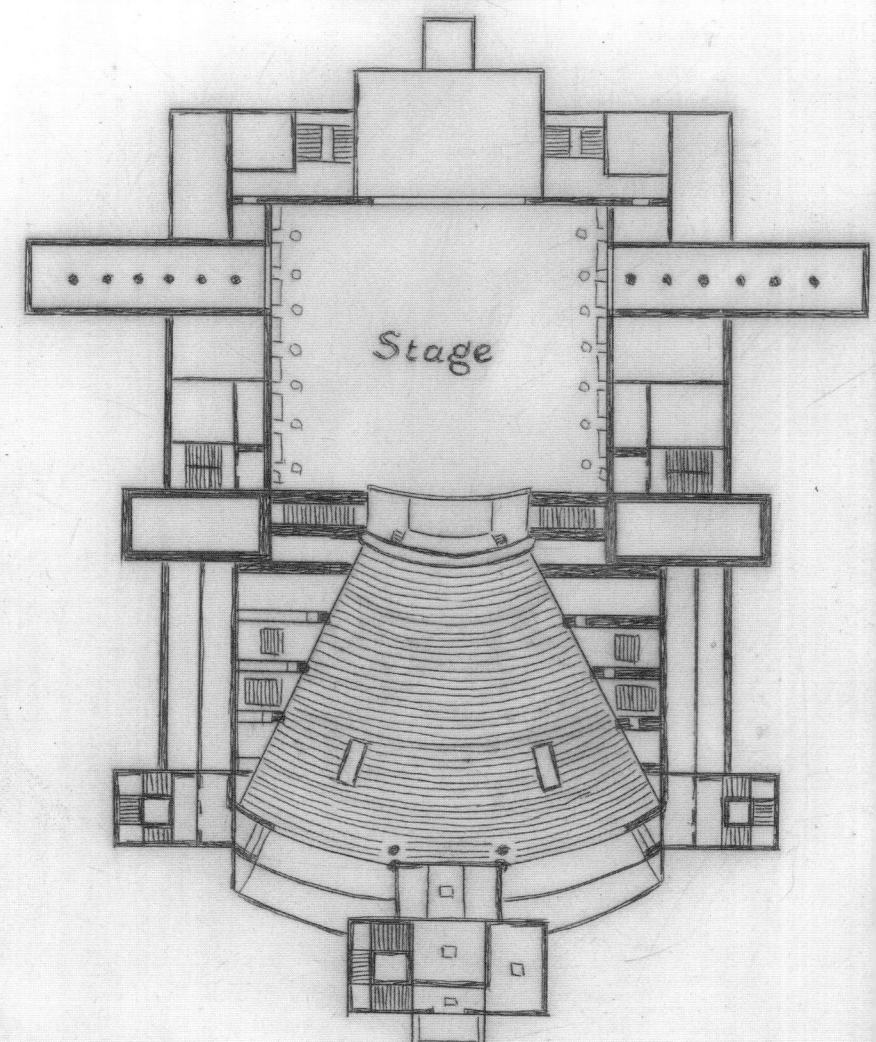

Stage

and then to ponder seriously with which quick movement of your body, sir, you are able to best symbolize a convulsion of the soul. The stage is the open, perceptible maw of poetry;

in your legs, dear sir, very specific states of
the soul can come to shuddering expression,
to say nothing of the face and the thousand
mimicking duties it has.

Your hair must obey you when, in order
to symbolize fright, it is supposed to
climb up into a mountain,

so that the spectators, the bankers and spice
traders, are frightened of you.

NOW THEN, you have been speechless; lost in thought you dug around in your nose like a naughty and reckless child, and now you start to speak.

But just when you want to do that, a fiery-green snake creeps and licks out of your pain-warped mouth, so that you yourself appear to tremble in all your limbs from horror.

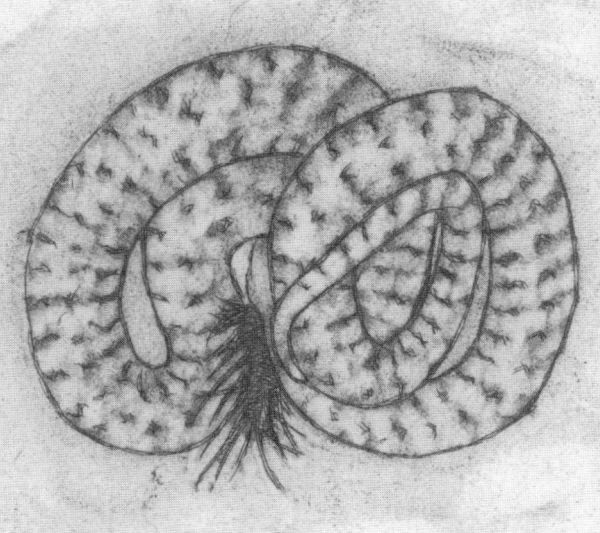

The snake falls to the ground and winds itself around the peaceful tuft of hair;

a cry of anguish traverses the entire
auditorium as if from a single mouth.

Indeed, now you are offering something new.

You stick a long, bent knife in one eye, so that the point of the knife appears underneath on the neck, near the throat, spurting out blood;

afterwards you light yourself a cigarette and do so especially cozily, as if you were secretly amused about something.

The blood that befouls your body turns into stars, and the stars dance beckoning, burning, and fierce around the whole stage area, while you catch them all with your open mouth, to make them disappear one by one. In this way your acting should have achieved a high degree of perfection.

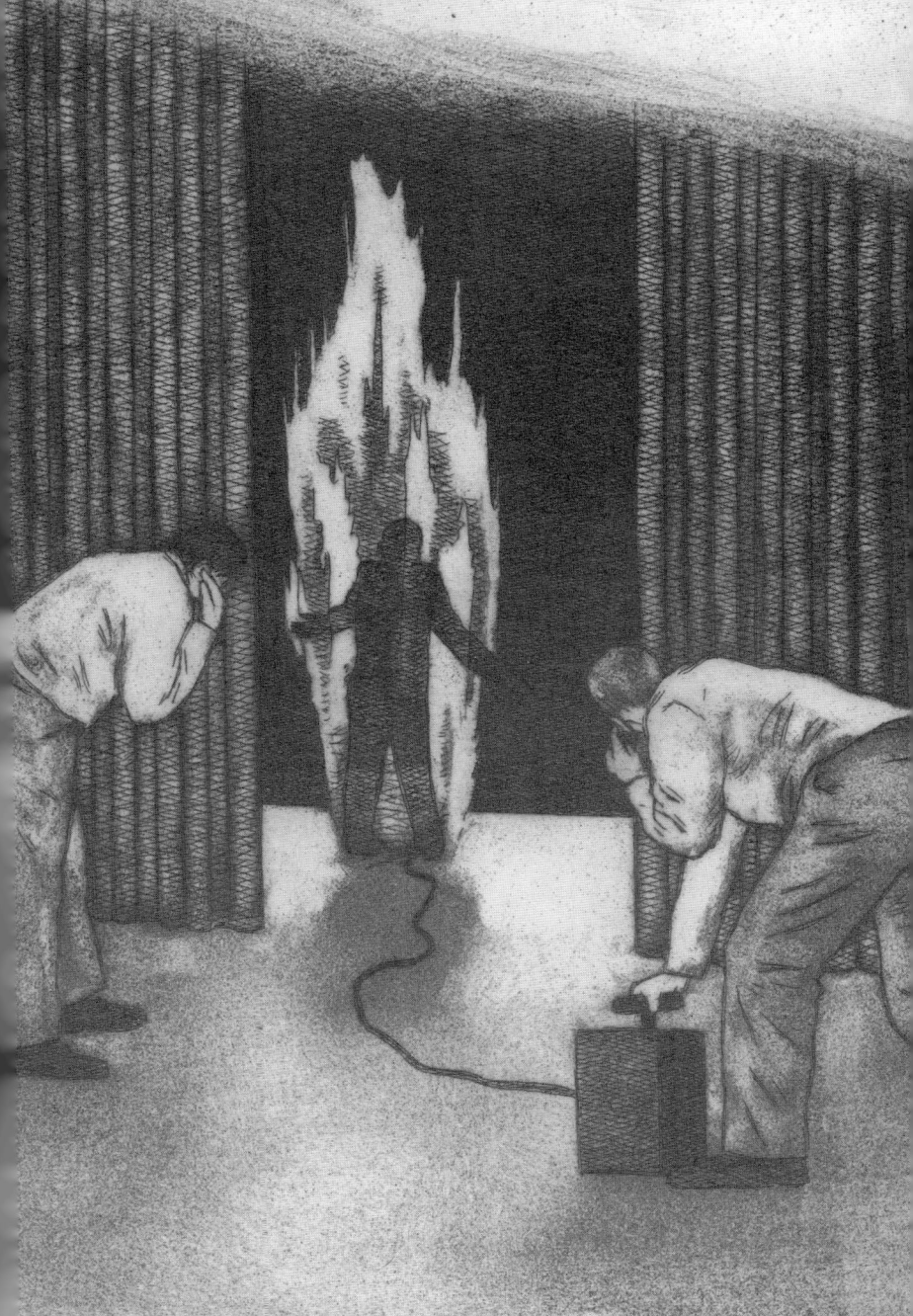

Then, the houses of the painted scenery topple
down like terrible drunkards and bury you.

Only your hand can be seen jutting out from under the steaming debris. The hand still moves a little, then the curtain falls.

TO THE READER:

SUCH A THING NEVER flitted across Job's honest brain: a period costume, some eye-liner and rouge to enthrall the inhabitants of Uz; a broadside, a poster, a spread in the paper. According to tradition, there was little for Job to advertise, to embellish, or to put on display. No room for art. Faced with the destruction of his world, he was, or so he thought, as true and natural a sufferer as he had been a prosperous landowner before. Scion of a good family and baron of all he saw, he even knows how to make his suffering profitable. He revels in the mud into which his God has thrown him, sucking the marrow from his misery, the only one on earth to earn such a privilege. It comes naturally to him; faith makes it easy, and that ease is fatal to his faith. Job loves his suffering, treasures it, suffers without feeling punished, confident in the endless beneficence of the universe, and this is why he utters no complaint—a blunder undoubtedly worse than sin, and the cautionary lesson of the book. Only God can be good and suffer at the same time. Mortals must be wicked, detest their condition, and howl over it.

YET IN JOB'S DRAMA special effects play a bigger role than one thinks. Props: a potsherd to scrape his sores, ashes to sit in. Pyrotechnics: the Sabeans attack with spears whirling, fire rains from the sky. Mechanics: hi-key lighting (the heights of heaven), sound-effects (voice from whirlwind), painted flats (endless burning desert). This apocalyptic dramaturgy has rarely been surpassed. One end of the world, however, is never enough. With every epoch a new end-time theater has to be built, different techniques for different publics.

JOB NEVER HAD TO ASK: is my hair right? Do I look good in this muddy bodysuit? The poor man was good, his suffering real, so real nobody believed it, then or now. Even the Almighty was incredulous. Why else would He refuse to answer the inquiry of his truest servant? Why else would He give the Accuser, *ha-satan*, a free hand to test him? Job never lost anything. The experience wasn't real; it was only a test. And who could tell if he did suffer? A touch of grease paint might have saved him, convinced his judges and, in turn, us.

IMAGINE YOU ARE an actor whose inspiration has run out. Night after night you play the same apocalypse with the same stale moans and tears. In Robert Walser's version of the Job legend an actor receives uproariously mundane advice. "To achieve a tragic effect one must seize both the nearest and the most extremely remote means." The nearest consists of the allotria of biological existence: hair and snot. The most remote is an indifferent universe that is exactly equal in coldness and grandeur to the petty passions of the victim, who, in contrast to the stars' brilliance, is so demeaned that he is altogether denied speech, even in the grand finale. In Walser's genre, speech belongs to the one who derides, not the one who suffers.

WHEN HIS WILL to suffer is broken and he finally learns to fear, Job has his losses instantly made good. He gets it all back, as Kafka says about Abraham, with interest. In a pantomime of suffering like Walser's, no one possesses anything to begin with; the stage is rented for the day. "This is the dreamlike effect, the true untruth, the stirring and last but not least the beautiful" appearance of the theater, Walser writes elsewhere. In this epigrammatic letter to an actor, contempt and sniggering replace fear and trembling; the cheap fakery of turn-of-the-century Berlin *Varieté* winks at us. And this does not diminish our pleasure. Quite the contrary—another kind of pleasure debuts here. We discover that one short step beyond drama farce awaits, pathos turns to pastiche, tragedy to travesty, and the eschatological exposes its clunky, obvious devices. Walser believed "the theater invests all its resources in frightening" the audience, yet this is not quite true of his writing. It tickles. A sweaty actor, low-paid flunky in the fear-making business, lumbers onstage, wig askew, to play the apocalypse.

WALSER'S TEXT was first published on February 28, 1907, in Siegfried Jacobsohn's Berlin theater journal *Die Schaubühne*. A century later, Friese Undine broadcasts it to the universe. Walser strove with his writing "to be small and stay small," as Jakob von Gunten puts it. Undine's engravings first of all pay homage to Walser's attraction to diminishment. Casual gestures, petty techniques, and cheap tricks abound. Then the illustrations do what Walser never dreamed: they project the actor's lesson onto a wider screen, turning up the hot lights, pushing beyond the half-filled house, fly-ropes, mirrors, and make-up—beyond the theatrical conditions of truth. If "the stage is the open, perceptible maw of poetry," illustrations are its teeth. "In a dream, the images that arise before the eye—whether or not it is the eye of the soul—have something sharp, something drawn very definitely," writes Walser in "The Theater, a Dream" (1907). Undine's images have this piercing definition. They develop a violent tendency in the text that might otherwise have been obscured by the reverence into which Walser's writing has recently fallen.

LLUSTRATING WALSER'S stories may be a more promising critical act than writing about them. No author in this period came so close to the comic book, to the caricature—except perhaps Kafka. Illustrations are naturally ironic. They abandon the language that they are supposed to depict, looking back at the word, shrunken by their exaggeration. In this way Walser's spare, aristocratic sentences find another distance from themselves in Undine's allusive engravings. It is the distance between the still gaslight-tinged show halls of burlesque and the fluorescent studios of television, between the actor and the social actor. In Undine's plates the scene plays before a meeting of stock-brokers fallen on hard times. The leading man is a middle manager in an insurance company, or a salesman, last of his breed, held upright by his suspenders. In the meantime, the technological basis for the show of suffering has only expanded and with it the possibilities for distribution. Scientists now stage-manage a cosmic spectacular that plays to the stars. And yet the tele-transmission is no triumph of progress. It does not seem to take place in the digital age, but in a previous analog one, whose gizmos are stuck together with string and tape.

WALSER CAME TO Berlin from Zurich in 1905, Undine to New York from Chicago in 2007. Upon arriving in the metropolis, each took aim at the establishments of ill-repute in which the muses had

taken refuge. Reducing tragedy to farce,
Walser exposed a dark side of the complicity
between theater and politics. Demoting art to
illustration, Undine rescues Walser's critical
gesture, mimics it and exaggerates it, at the
same time reviving the genre of the illustrated
book last practiced with such political insight
by Frans Masereel and with such an ability to
transmute our fantasies by Bruno Schulz.

IN FRIESE UNDINE'S engravings, Walser's
insight shines, what Job never admits:
suffering released from the need to hate it—
under certain conditions—is mirth.

— PAUL NORTH

ANSWER TO AN INQUIRY / ROBERT WALSER

Copyright © 2010 by Paul North and Friese Undine

The translation is based on the following German publication:
Walser, Robert. "Beantwortung einer Anfrage." *Die Schaubühne*.
28 Feb 1907: 236-7.

ISBN 978-1-933254-74-6
First Edition, 2010
Ugly Duckling Presse, 232 Third Street, Brooklyn, NY 11215
Distributed by Small Press Distribution: www.spdbooks.org

Published with the generous support of the
Consulate General of Switzerland in New York.

Design: Don't Look Now!
Type: Warnock & Gill Sans

Printed in the United States by Thomson-Shore on acid-free,
FSC-certified paper and bound in cloth-covered boards in an
edition of one thousand copies. The first seventy-five copies are
signed and numbered by the translator and the artist.